NINE
STORIES

Nine Stories

Kate Chopin

COUNTERPOINT
Berkeley, California

COUNTERPOINTS 9

NINE STORIES

First Counterpoint Edition: 2022

ISBN: 978-1-64009-574-8

The Library of Congress Cataloging-in-Publication Data is available.

Series cover designed by Jenny Carrow
Cover designed by Lexi Earle
Series interior designed by Jordan Koluch
Book designed by Laura Berry

COUNTERPOINT
2560 Ninth Street, Suite 318
Berkeley, CA 94710
www.counterpointpress.com

Printed in the United States of America

10 9 8 7 6 5 4 3 2 1

Contents

NINE
STORIES

BEYOND THE BAYOU

The bayou curved like a crescent around the point of land on which La Folle's cabin stood. Between the stream and the hut lay a big abandoned field, where cattle were pastured when the bayou supplied them with water enough. Through the woods that spread back into unknown regions the woman had drawn an imaginary line, and past this circle she never stepped. This was the form of her only mania.

She was now a large, gaunt black woman, past thirty-five. Her real name was Jacqueline, but every one on the plantation called her La Folle, because in childhood she had been frightened literally "out of her senses," and had never wholly regained them.

It was when there had been skirmishing and sharpshooting all day in the woods. Evening was near when P'tit Maître, black with powder and crimson with blood, had staggered into the cabin of Jacqueline's mother, his pursuers close at his heels. The sight had stunned her childish reason.

She dwelt alone in her solitary cabin, for the rest of the quarters had long since been removed beyond her sight and knowledge. She had more physical strength than most men, and made her patch of cotton and corn and tobacco like the best of them. But of the world beyond the bayou she had long known nothing, save what her morbid fancy conceived.

People at Bellissime had grown used to

her and her way, and they thought nothing of it. Even when "Old Mis'" died, they did not wonder that La Folle had not crossed the bayou, but had stood upon her side of it, wailing and lamenting.

P'tit Maître was now the owner of Bellissime. He was a middle-aged man, with a family of beautiful daughters about him, and a little son whom La Folle loved as if he had been her own. She called him Chéri, and so did every one else because she did.

None of the girls had ever been to her what Chéri was. They had each and all loved to be with her, and to listen to her wondrous stories of things that always happened "yonda, beyon' de bayou."

But none of them had stroked her black hand quite as Chéri did, nor rested their heads against her knee so confidingly, nor fallen asleep in her arms as he used to do. For Chéri hardly did such things now, since he had become the proud possessor of a gun, and had had his black curls cut off.

That summer—the summer Chéri gave La Folle two black curls tied with a knot of red ribbon—the water ran so low in the bayou that even the little children at Bellissime were able to cross it on foot, and the cattle were sent to pasture down by the river. La Folle was sorry when they were gone, for she loved these dumb companions well, and liked to feel that they were there, and to hear them browsing by night up to her own inclosure.

It was Saturday afternoon, when the fields were deserted. The men had flocked to a neighboring village to do their week's trading, and the women were occupied with household affairs,—La Folle as well as the others. It was then she mended and washed her handful of clothes, scoured her house, and did her baking.

In this last employment she never forgot Chéri. To-day she had fashioned croquignoles of the most fantastic and alluring shapes for him. So when she saw the boy come trudging across the old field with his gleaming little new rifle on his shoulder, she called out gayly to him, "Chéri! Chéri!"

But Chéri did not need the summons, for he was coming straight to her. His pockets all bulged out with almonds and raisins and an orange that he had secured for her from the very fine dinner which had been given that day up at his father's house.

He was a sunny-faced youngster of ten. When he had emptied his pockets, La Folle patted his round red cheek, wiped his soiled hands on her apron, and smoothed his hair. Then she watched him as, with his cakes in his hand, he crossed her strip of cotton back of the cabin, and disappeared into the wood.

He had boasted of the things he was going to do with his gun out there.

"You think they got plenty deer in the wood, La Folle?" he had inquired, with the calculating air of an experienced hunter.

"*Non, non!*" the woman laughed. "Don't you look fo' no deer, Chéri. Dat's too big. But you bring La Folle one good fat squirrel fo' her dinner to-morrow, an' she goin' be satisfi'."

"One squirrel ain't a bite. I'll bring you mo' 'an one, La Folle," he had boasted pompously as he went away.

When the woman, an hour later, heard the report of the boy's rifle close to the wood's edge, she would have thought nothing of it if a sharp cry of distress had not followed the sound.

She withdrew her arms from the tub of suds in which they had been plunged, dried them upon her apron, and as quickly as her trembling limbs would bear her, hurried to the spot whence the ominous report had come.

It was as she feared. There she found Chéri stretched upon the ground, with his rifle beside him. He moaned piteously:—

"I'm dead, La Folle! I'm dead! I'm gone!"

"*Non, non!*" she exclaimed resolutely, as she knelt beside him. "Put you' arm 'roun' La Folle's nake, Chéri. Dat's nuttin'; dat goin' be nuttin'." She lifted him in her powerful arms.

Chéri had carried his gun muzzle-downward. He had stumbled,—he did not know how. He only knew that he had a ball lodged somewhere in his leg, and he thought that his end was at hand. Now, with his head upon the woman's shoulder, he moaned and wept with pain and fright.

"Oh, La Folle! La Folle! it hurt so bad! I can' stan' it, La Folle!"

"Don't cry, *mon bébé, mon bébé, mon Chéri*!" the woman spoke soothingly as she covered the ground with long strides. "La Folle goin' mine you; Doctor Bonfils goin' come make *mon Chéri* well agin."

She had reached the abandoned field. As she crossed it with her precious burden, she looked constantly and restlessly from side to side. A terrible fear was upon her,—the fear of the world beyond the bayou, the morbid and insane dread she had been under since childhood.

When she was at the bayou's edge she stood there, and shouted for help as if a life depended upon it:—

"Oh, P'tit Maître! Venez donc! Au secours! Au secours!"

No voice responded. Chéri's hot tears were scalding her neck. She called for each and every one upon the place, and still no answer came.

She shouted, she wailed; but whether her voice remained unheard or unheeded, no reply came to her frenzied cries. And all the while Chéri moaned and wept and entreated to be taken home to his mother.

La Folle gave a last despairing look around her. Extreme terror was upon her. She clasped the child close against her breast, where he could feel her heart beat like a muffled hammer. Then shutting her eyes, she ran suddenly down the shallow bank of the bayou, and never stopped till she had climbed the opposite shore.

She stood there quivering an instant as she opened her eyes. Then she plunged into the footpath through the trees.

She spoke no more to Chéri, but muttered constantly, "Bon Dien, ayez pitié La Folle! Bon Dieu, ayez pitié moi!"

Instinct seemed to guide her. When the pathway spread clear and smooth enough before her, she again closed her eyes tightly against the sight of that unknown and terrifying world.

A child, playing in some weeds, caught sight of her as she neared the quarters. The little one uttered a cry of dismay.

"La Folle!" she screamed, in her piercing treble. "La Folle done cross de bayer!"

Quickly the cry passed down the line of cabins.

"Yonda, La Folle done cross de bayou!"

Children, old men, old women, young ones with infants in their arms, flocked to doors and windows to see this awe-inspiring spectacle. Most of them shuddered with superstitious dread of what it might portend. "She totin' Chéri!" some of them shouted.

Some of the more daring gathered about her, and followed at her heels, only to fall back with new terror when she turned her distorted face upon them. Her eyes were bloodshot and the saliva had gathered in a white foam on her black lips.

Some one had run ahead of her to where P'tit Maître sat with his family and guests upon the gallery.

"P'tit Maître! La Folle done cross de bayou! Look her! Look her yonda totin' Chéri!" This startling intimation was the first which they had of the woman's approach.

She was now near at hand. She walked with long strides. Her eyes were fixed desperately before her, and she breathed heavily, as a tired ox.

At the foot of the stairway, which she could not have mounted, she laid the boy in his father's arms. Then the world that had looked red to La Folle suddenly turned black,—like that day she had seen powder and blood.

She reeled for an instant. Before a sustaining arm could reach her, she fell heavily to the ground.

When La Folle regained consciousness, she was at home again, in her own cabin and upon her own bed. The moon rays, streaming in through the open door and windows, gave what light was needed to the old black mammy who stood at the table concocting a tisane of fragrant herbs. It was very late.

Others who had come, and found that the stupor clung to her, had gone again. P'tit Maître had been there, and with him Doctor Bonfils, who said that La Folle might die.

But death had passed her by. The voice was very clear and steady with which she spoke to Tante Lizette, brewing her tisane there in a corner.

"Ef you will give me one good drink tisane, Tante Lizette, I b'lieve I'm goin' sleep, me."

And she did sleep; so soundly, so health-fully, that old Lizette without compunction stole softly away, to creep back through the moonlit fields to her own cabin in the new quarters.

The first touch of the cool gray morning awoke La Folle. She arose, calmly, as if no tempest had shaken and threatened her existence but yesterday.

She donned her new blue cottonade and white apron, for she remembered that this was Sunday. When she had made for herself a cup of strong black coffee, and drunk it with relish, she quitted the cabin and walked across the old familiar field to the bayou's edge again.

She did not stop there as she had always done before, but crossed with a long, steady stride as if she had done this all her life.

When she had made her way through the brush and scrub cottonwood-trees that lined the opposite bank, she found herself upon the border of a field where the white, bursting cotton, with the dew upon it, gleamed for acres and acres like frosted silver in the early dawn.

La Folle drew a long, deep breath as she gazed across the country. She walked slowly and uncertainly, like one who hardly knows how, looking about her as she went.

The cabins, that yesterday had sent a clamor of voices to pursue her, were quiet now. No one was yet astir at Bellissime. Only the birds that darted here and there from hedges were awake, and singing their matins.

When La Folle came to the broad stretch of velvety lawn that surrounded the house, she moved slowly and with delight over the springy turf, that was delicious beneath her tread.

She stopped to find whence came those

perfumes that were assailing her senses with memories from a time far gone.

There they were, stealing up to her from the thousand blue violets that peeped out from green, luxuriant beds. There they were, showering down from the big waxen bells of the magnolias far above her head, and from the jessamine clumps around her.

There were roses, too, without number. To right and left palms spread in broad and graceful curves. It all looked like enchantment beneath the sparkling sheen of dew.

When La Folle had slowly and cautiously mounted the many steps that led up to the veranda, she turned to look back at the perilous ascent she had made. Then she caught sight of the river, bending like a silver bow at the foot of Bellissime. Exultation possessed her soul.

La Folle rapped softly upon a door near at hand. Chéri's mother soon cautiously opened it. Quickly and cleverly she dissembled the astonishment she felt at seeing La Folle.

"Ah, La Folle! Is it you, so early?"

"*Oui*, madame. I come ax how my po' li'le Chéri to, 's mo'nin'."

"He is feeling easier, thank you, La Folle. Doctor Bonfils says it will be nothing serious. He's sleeping now. Will you come back when he awakes?"

"*Non*, madame. I'm goin' wait yair tell Chéri wake up." La Folle seated herself upon the topmost step of the veranda.

A look of wonder and deep content crept into her face as she watched for the first time the sun rise upon the new, the beautiful world beyond the bayou.

DÉSIRÉE'S BABY

As the day was pleasant, Madame Valmondé drove over to L'Abri to see Désirée and the baby.

It made her laugh to think of Désirée with a baby. Why, it seemed but yesterday that Désirée was little more than a baby herself; when Monsieur in riding through the gateway of Valmondé had found her lying asleep in the shadow of the big stone pillar.

The little one awoke in his arms and began to cry for "Dada." That was as much as she could do or say. Some people thought she might have strayed there of her own accord, for she was of the toddling age. The prevailing belief was that she had been purposely left by a party of Texans, whose canvas-covered wagon, late in the day, had crossed the ferry that Coton Maïs kept, just below the plantation. In time Madame Valmondé abandoned every speculation but the one that Désirée had been sent to her by a beneficent Providence to be the child of her affection, seeing that she was without child of the flesh. For the girl grew to be beautiful and gentle, affectionate and sincere,—the idol of Valmondé.

It was no wonder, when she stood one day against the stone pillar in whose shadow she had lain asleep, eighteen years before, that Armand Aubigny riding by and seeing her there, had fallen in love with her. That was the way all the Aubignys fell in love, as if struck by a pistol shot. The wonder was that he had not loved her before; for he had known her since his father brought him home from Paris, a boy of eight, after his mother died there. The passion that awoke in him that day, when he saw her at the gate, swept along like an avalanche, or like a prairie fire, or like anything that drives headlong over all obstacles.

Monsieur Valmondé grew practical and wanted things well considered: that is, the girl's obscure origin. Armand looked into her eyes and did not care. He was reminded that she was nameless. What did it matter about a name when he could give her one of the oldest and proudest in Louisiana? He ordered the *corbeille* from Paris, and contained himself with what patience he could until it arrived; then they were married.

Madame Valmondé had not seen Désirée and the baby for four weeks. When she reached L'Abri she shuddered at the first sight of it, as she always did. It was a sad looking place, which for many years had not known the gentle presence of a mistress, old Monsieur Aubigny having married and buried his wife in France, and she having loved her own land too well ever to leave it. The roof came down steep and black like a cowl, reaching out beyond the wide galleries that encircled the yellow stuccoed house. Big, solemn oaks grew close to it, and their thick-leaved, far-reaching branches shadowed it like a pall. Young Aubigny's rule was a strict one, too, and under it his negroes had forgotten how to be gay, as they had been during the old master's easy-going and indulgent lifetime.

The young mother was recovering slowly, and lay full length, in her soft white muslins and laces, upon a couch. The baby was beside her, upon her arm, where he had fallen asleep, at her breast. The yellow nurse woman sat beside a window fanning herself.

Madame Valmondé bent her portly figure over Désirée and kissed her, holding her an instant tenderly in her arms. Then she turned to the child.

"This is not the baby!" she exclaimed, in startled tones. French was the language spoken at Valmondé in those days.

"I knew you would be astonished," laughed Désirée, "at the way he has grown. The little *cochon de lait*! Look at his legs, mamma, and his hands and finger-nails,— real finger-nails. Zandrine had to cut them this morning. Isn't it true, Zandrine?"

The woman bowed her turbaned head majestically, "Mais si, Madame."

"And the way he cries," went on Désirée, "is deafening. Armand heard him the other day as far away as La Blanche's cabin."

Madame Valmondé had never removed

her eyes from the child. She lifted it and walked with it over to the window that was lightest. She scanned the baby narrowly, then looked as searchingly at Zandrine, whose face was turned to gaze across the fields.

"Yes, the child has grown, has changed," said Madame Valmondé, slowly, as she replaced it beside its mother. "What does Armand say?"

Désirée's face became suffused with a glow that was happiness itself.

"Oh, Armand is the proudest father in the parish, I believe, chiefly because it is a boy, to bear his name; though he says not,— that he would have loved a girl as well. But I know it isn't true. I know he says that to please me. And mamma," she added, drawing Madame Valmondé's head down to her, and speaking in a whisper, "he hasn't punished one of them—not one of them—since baby is born. Even Négrillon, who pretended to have burnt his leg that he might rest from work—he only laughed, and said Négrillon was a great scamp. Oh, mamma, I'm so happy; it frightens me."

What Désirée said was true. Marriage, and later the birth of his son, had softened Armand Aubigny's imperious and exacting nature greatly. This was what made the gentle Désirée so happy, for she loved him desperately. When he frowned she trembled, but loved him. When he smiled, she asked no greater blessing of God. But Armand's dark, handsome face had not often been disfigured by frowns since the day he fell in love with her.

When the baby was about three months old, Désirée awoke one day to the conviction that there was something in the air menacing her peace. It was at first too subtle to grasp. It had only been a disquieting suggestion; an air of mystery among the blacks; unexpected visits from far-off neighbors who could hardly account for their coming. Then a strange, an awful change in her husband's manner, which she dared not ask him to explain. When he spoke to her, it was with averted eyes, from which the old love-light seemed to have gone out. He absented himself from home; and when there, avoided her presence and that of her child, without excuse. And the very spirit of Satan seemed suddenly to take hold of him in his dealings with the slaves. Désirée was miserable enough to die.

She sat in her room, one hot afternoon, in her *peignoir*, listlessly drawing through her fingers the strands of her long, silky brown hair that hung about her shoulders. The baby, half naked, lay asleep upon her own great mahogany bed, that was like a sumptuous throne, with its satin-lined half-canopy. One of La Blanche's little quadroon boys—half naked too—stood fanning the child slowly with a fan of peacock feathers. Désirée's eyes had been fixed absently and sadly upon the baby, while she was striving to penetrate the threatening mist that she felt closing about her. She looked from her child to the boy who stood beside him, and back again; over and over. "Ah!" It was a cry that she could not help; which she was not conscious of having uttered. The blood turned like ice in her veins, and a clammy moisture gathered upon her face.

She tried to speak to the little quadroon boy; but no sound would come, at first. When he heard his name uttered, he looked up, and his mistress was pointing to the door. He laid aside the great, soft fan, and obediently stole away, over the polished floor, on his bare tiptoes.

She stayed motionless, with gaze riveted

upon her child, and her face the picture of fright.

Presently her husband entered the room, and without noticing her, went to a table and began to search among some papers which covered it.

"Armand," she called to him, in a voice which must have stabbed him, if he was human. But he did not notice. "Armand," she said again. Then she rose and tottered towards him. "Armand," she panted once more, clutching his arm, "look at our child. What does it mean? tell me."

He coldly but gently loosened her fingers from about his arm and thrust the hand away from him. "Tell me what it means!" she cried despairingly.

"It means," he answered lightly, "that the child is not white; it means that you are not white."

A quick conception of all that this

accusation meant for her nerved her with unwonted courage to deny it. "It is a lie; it is not true, I am white! Look at my hair, it is brown; and my eyes are gray, Armand, you know they are gray. And my skin is fair," seizing his wrist. "Look at my hand; whiter than yours, Armand," she laughed hysterically.

"As white as La Blanche's," he returned cruelly; and went away leaving her alone with their child.

When she could hold a pen in her hand, she sent a despairing letter to Madame Valmondé.

"My mother, they tell me I am not white. Armand has told me I am not white. For God's sake tell them it is not true. You must know it is not true. I shall die. I must die. I cannot be so unhappy, and live."

The answer that came was as brief:

"My own Désirée: Come home to

Valmondé; back to your mother who loves you. Come with your child."

When the letter reached Désirée she went with it to her husband's study, and laid it open upon the desk before which he sat. She was like a stone image: silent, white, motionless after she placed it there.

In silence he ran his cold eyes over the written words. He said nothing. "Shall I go, Armand?" she asked in tones sharp with agonized suspense.

"Yes, go."

"Do you want me to go?"

"Yes, I want you to go."

He thought Almighty God had dealt cruelly and unjustly with him; and felt, somehow, that he was paying Him back in kind when he stabbed thus into his wife's soul. Moreover he no longer loved her, because of the unconscious injury she had brought upon his home and his name.

She turned away like one stunned by a blow, and walked slowly towards the door, hoping he would call her back.

"Good-by, Armand," she moaned.

He did not answer her. That was his last blow at fate.

Désirée went in search of her child. Zandrine was pacing the sombre gallery with it. She took the little one from the nurse's arms with no word of explanation, and descending the steps, walked away, under the live-oak branches.

It was an October afternoon; the sun was just sinking. Out in the still fields the negroes were picking cotton.

Désirée had not changed the thin white garment nor the slippers which she wore. Her hair was uncovered and the sun's rays brought a golden gleam from its brown meshes. She did not take the broad, beaten road which led to the far-off plantation of

Valmondé. She walked across a deserted field, where the stubble bruised her tender feet, so delicately shod, and tore her thin gown to shreds.

She disappeared among the reeds and willows that grew thick along the banks of the deep, sluggish bayou; and she did not come back again.

Some weeks later there was a curious scene enacted at L'Abri. In the centre of the smoothly swept back yard was a great bonfire. Armand Aubigny sat in the wide hallway that commanded a view of the spectacle; and it was he who dealt out to a half dozen negroes the material which kept this fire ablaze.

A graceful cradle of willow, with all its dainty furbishings, was laid upon the pyre, which had already been fed with the richness of a priceless *layette*. Then there were silk gowns, and velvet and satin ones added to these; laces, too, and embroideries; bonnets and gloves; for the *corbeille* had been of rare quality.

The last thing to go was a tiny bundle of letters; innocent little scribblings that Désirée had sent to him during the days of their espousal. There was the remnant of one back in the drawer from which he took them. But it was not Désirée's; it was part of an old letter from his mother to his father. He read it. She was thanking God for the blessing of her husband's love:—

"But, above all," she wrote, "night and day, I thank the good God for having so arranged our lives that our dear Armand will never know that his mother, who adores him, belongs to the race that is cursed with the brand of slavery."

A RESPECTABLE
WOMAN

Mrs. Baroda was a little provoked to
learn that her husband expected his
friend, Gouvernail, up to spend a week or
two on the plantation.

They had entertained a good deal during
the winter; much of the time had also been
passed in New Orleans in various forms of
mild dissipation. She was looking forward
to a period of unbroken rest, now, and
undisturbed tête-a-tête with her husband,
when he informed her that Gouvernail was
coming up to stay a week or two.

This was a man she had heard much of but never seen. He had been her husband's college friend; was now a journalist, and in no sense a society man or "a man about town," which were, perhaps, some of the reasons she had never met him. But she had unconsciously formed an image of him in her mind. She pictured him tall, slim, cynical; with eye-glasses, and his hands in his pockets; and she did not like him. Gouvernail was slim enough, but he wasn't very tall nor very cynical; neither did he wear eye-glasses nor carry his hands in his pockets. And she rather liked him when he first presented himself.

But why she liked him she could not explain satisfactorily to herself when she partly attempted to do so. She could discover in him none of those brilliant and promising traits which Gaston, her husband, had often assured her that he possessed. On the contrary, he sat rather mute and receptive before her chatty eagerness to make him feel at home and in face of Gaston's frank and wordy hospitality. His manner was as courteous toward her as the most exacting woman could require; but he made no direct appeal to her approval or even esteem.

Once settled at the plantation he seemed to like to sit upon the wide portico in the shade of one of the big Corinthian pillars, smoking his cigar lazily and listening attentively to Gaston's experience as a sugar planter.

"This is what I call living," he would utter with deep satisfaction, as the air that swept across the sugar field caressed him with its warm and scented velvety touch. It pleased him also to get on familiar terms with the big dogs that came about him, rubbing themselves sociably against his legs.

He did not care to fish, and displayed no eagerness to go out and kill grosbecs when Gaston proposed doing so.

Gouvernail's personality puzzled Mrs. Baroda, but she liked him. Indeed, he was a lovable, inoffensive fellow. After a few days, when she could understand him no better than at first, she gave over being puzzled and remained piqued. In this mood she left her husband and her guest, for the most part, alone together. Then finding that Gouvernail took no manner of exception to her action, she imposed her society upon him, accompanying him in his idle strolls to the mill and walks along the batture. She persistently sought to penetrate the reserve in which he had unconsciously enveloped himself.

"When is he going—your friend?" she one day asked her husband. "For my part, he tires me frightfully."

"Not for a week yet, dear. I can't understand; he gives you no trouble."

"No. I should like him better if he did; if he were more like others, and I had to plan somewhat for his comfort and enjoyment."

Gaston took his wife's pretty face between his hands and looked tenderly and laughingly into her troubled eyes. They were making a bit of toilet sociably together in Mrs. Baroda's dressing-room.

"You are full of surprises, ma belle," he said to her. "Even I can never count upon how you are going to act under given conditions." He kissed her and turned to fasten his cravat before the mirror.

"Here you are," he went on, "taking poor Gouvernail seriously and making a commotion over him, the last thing he would desire or expect."

"Commotion!" she hotly resented. "Nonsense! How can you say such a thing?

Commotion, indeed! But, you know, you said he was clever."

"So he is. But the poor fellow is run down by overwork now. That's why I asked him here to take a rest."

"You used to say he was a man of ideas," she retorted, unconciliated. "I expected him to be interesting, at least. I'm going to the city in the morning to have my spring gowns fitted. Let me know when Mr. Gouvernail is gone; I shall be at my Aunt Octavie's."

That night she went and sat alone upon a bench that stood beneath a live oak tree at the edge of the gravel walk.

She had never known her thoughts or her intentions to be so confused. She could gather nothing from them but the feeling of a distinct necessity to quit her home in the morning.

Mrs. Baroda heard footsteps crunching the gravel; but could discern in the darkness only the approaching red point of a lighted cigar. She knew it was Gouvernail, for her husband did not smoke. She hoped to remain unnoticed, but her white gown revealed her to him. He threw away his cigar and seated himself upon the bench beside her; without a suspicion that she might object to his presence.

"Your husband told me to bring this to you, Mrs. Baroda," he said, handing her a filmy, white scarf with which she sometimes enveloped her head and shoulders. She accepted the scarf from him with a murmur of thanks, and let it lie in her lap.

He made some commonplace observation upon the baneful effect of the night air at that season. Then as his gaze reached out into the darkness, he murmured, half to himself:

"'Night of south winds—night of the large few stars! Still nodding night——'"

She made no reply to this apostrophe to the night, which indeed, was not addressed to her.

Gouvernail was in no sense a diffident man, for he was not a self-conscious one. His periods of reserve were not constitutional, but the result of moods. Sitting there beside Mrs. Baroda, his silence melted for the time.

He talked freely and intimately in a low, hesitating drawl that was not unpleasant to hear. He talked of the old college days when he and Gaston had been a good deal to each other; of the days of keen and blind ambitions and large intentions. Now there was left with him, at least, a philosophic acquiescence to the existing order—only a desire to be permitted to exist, with now and then a little whiff of genuine life, such as he was breathing now.

Her mind only vaguely grasped what he

was saying. Her physical being was for the moment predominant. She was not thinking of his words, only drinking in the tones of his voice. She wanted to reach out her hand in the darkness and touch him with the sensitive tips of her fingers upon the face or the lips. She wanted to draw close to him and whisper against his cheek—she did not care what—as she might have done if she had not been a respectable woman.

The stronger the impulse grew to bring herself near him, the further, in fact, did she draw away from him. As soon as she could do so without an appearance of too great rudeness, she rose and left him there alone.

Before she reached the house, Gouvernail had lighted a fresh cigar and ended his apostrophe to the night.

Mrs. Baroda was greatly tempted that night to tell her husband—who was also her friend—of this folly that had seized her. But she did not yield to the temptation. Beside being a respectable woman she was a very sensible one; and she knew there are some battles in life which a human being must fight alone.

When Gaston arose in the morning, his wife had already departed. She had taken an early morning train to the city. She did not return till Gouvernail was gone from under her roof.

There was some talk of having him back during the summer that followed. That is, Gaston greatly desired it; but this desire yielded to his wife's strenuous opposition.

However, before the year ended, she proposed, wholly from herself, to have Gouvernail visit them again. Her husband was surprised and delighted with the suggestion coming from her.

"I am glad, chère amie, to know that

you have finally overcome your dislike for him; truly he did not deserve it."

"Oh," she told him, laughingly, after pressing a long, tender kiss upon his lips, "I have overcome everything! you will see. This time I shall be very nice to him."

WISER THAN A GOD

To love and be wise is scarcely
granted even to a god.

—*LATIN PROVERB*.

Y ou might at least show some distaste
for the task, Paula," said Mrs. Von
Stoltz, in her querulous invalid voice, to
her daughter who stood before the glass
bestowing a few final touches of embellish-
ment upon an otherwise plain toilet.

"And to what purpose, Mutterchen?
The task is not entirely to my liking, I'll ad-
mit; but there can be no question as to its

results, which you even must concede are gratifying."

"Well, it's not the career your poor father had in view for you. How often he has told me when I complained that you were kept too closely at work, 'I want that Paula shall be at the head,'" with appealing look through the window and up into the gray, November sky into that far "somewhere," which might be the abode of her departed husband.

"It isn't a career at all, mamma; it's only a make-shift," answered the girl, noting the happy effect of an amber pin that she had thrust through the coils of her lustrous yellow hair. "The pot must be kept boiling at all hazards, pending the appearance of that hoped for career. And you forget that an occasion like this gives me the very opportunities I want."

"I can't see the advantages of bringing

your talent down to such banale servitude. Who are those people, anyway?"

The mother's question ended in a cough which shook her into speechless exhaustion.

"Ah! I have let you sit too long by the window, mother," said Paula, hastening to wheel the invalid's chair nearer the grate fire that was throwing genial light and warmth into the room, turning its plainness to beauty as by a touch of enchantment. "By the way," she added, having arranged her mother as comfortably as might be, "I haven't yet qualified for that 'banale servitude,' as you call it." And approaching the piano which stood in a distant alcove of the room, she took up a roll of music that lay curled up on the instrument, straightened it out before her. Then, seeming to remember the question which her mother had asked, turned on the stool to answer it. "Don't you know?

The Brainards, very swell people, and awfully rich. The daughter is that girl whom I once told you about, having gone to the Conservatory to cultivate her voice and old Engfelder told her in his brusque way to go back home, that his system was not equal to overcoming impossibilities."

"Oh, those people."

"Yes; this little party is given in honor of the son's return from Yale or Harvard, or some place or other." And turning to the piano she softly ran over the dances, whilst the mother gazed into the fire with unresigned sadness, which the bright music seemed to deepen.

"Well, there'll be no trouble about *that*," said Paula, with comfortable assurance, having ended the last waltz. "There's nothing here to tempt me into flights of originality; there'll be no difficulty in keeping to the hand-organ effect."

"Don't leave me with those dreadful impressions, Paula; my poor nerves are on edge."

"You are too hard on the dances, mamma. There are certain strains here and there that I thought not bad."

"It's your youth that finds it so; I have outlived such illusions."

"What an inconsistent little mother it is!" the girl exclaimed, laughing. "You told me only yesterday it was my youth that was so impatient with the commonplace happenings of everyday life. That age, needing to seek its delights, finds them often in unsuspected places, wasn't that it?"

"Don't chatter, Paula; some music, some music!"

"What shall it be?" asked Paula, touching a succession of harmonious chords. "It must be short."

"The 'Berceuse,' then; Chopin's. But

soft, soft and a little slowly as your dear father used to play it."

Mrs. Von Stoltz leaned her head back amongst the cushions, and with eyes closed, drank in the wonderful strains that came like an ethereal voice out of the past, lulling her spirit into the quiet of sweet memories.

When the last soft notes had melted into silence, Paula approached her mother and looking into the pale face saw that tears stood beneath the closed eyelids. "Ah! mamma, I have made you unhappy," she cried, in distress.

"No, my child; you have given me a joy that you don't dream of. I have no more pain. Your music has done for me what Farinelli's singing did for poor King Philip of Spain; it has cured me."

There was a glow of pleasure on the warm face and the eyes with almost the brightness of health. "Whilst I listened to you, Paula, my soul went out from me and lived again through an evening long ago. We were in our pretty room at Leipsic. The soft air and the moonlight came through the open-curtained window, making a quivering fret-work along the gleaming waxed floor. You lay in my arms and I felt again the pressure of your warm, plump little body against me. Your father was at the piano playing the 'Berceuse,' and all at once you drew my head down and whispered, 'Ist es nicht wonderschen, mamma?' When it ended, you were sleeping and your father took you from my arms and laid you gently in bed."

Paula knelt beside her mother, holding the frail hands which she kissed tenderly.

"Now you must go, liebchen. Ring for Berta, she will do all that is needed. I feel very strong to night. But do not come back too late."

"I shall be home as early as possible;

likely in the last car, I couldn't stay longer or I should have to walk. You know the house in case there should be need to send for me?"

"Yes, yes; but there will be no need."

Paula kissed her mother lovingly and went out into the drear November night with the roll of dances under her arm.

II

THE DOOR OF the stately mansion at which Paula rang, was opened by a footman, who invited her to "kindly walk upstairs."

"Show the young lady into the music room, James," called from some upper region a voice, doubtless the same whose impossibilities had been so summarily dealt with by Herr Engfelder, and Paula was led through a suite of handsome apartments, the warmth and mellow light of which were very grateful, after the chill out-door air.

Once in the music room, she removed her wraps and seated herself comfortably to await developments. Before her stood the magnificent "Steinway," on which her eyes rested with greedy admiration, and her fingers twitched with a desire to awaken its inviting possibilities. The odor of flowers impregnated the air like a subtle intoxicant and over everything hung a quiet smile of expectancy, disturbed by an occasional feminine flutter above stairs, or muffled suggestions of distant household sounds.

Presently, a young man entered the drawing-room,—no doubt, the college student, for he looked critically and with an air of proprietorship at the festive arrangements, venturing the bestowal of a few improving touches. Then, gazing with pardonable complacency at his own handsome, athletic figure in the mirror, he saw reflected Paula looking at him, with a demure smile lighting her blue eyes.

"By Jove!" was his startled exclamation. Then, approaching, "I beg pardon, Miss—Miss—"

"Von Stoltz."

"Miss Von Stoltz," drawing the right conclusion from her simple toilet and the roll of music. "I hadn't seen you when I came in. Have you been here long? and sitting all alone, too? That's certainly rough."

"Oh, I've been here but a few moments, and was very well entertained."

"I dare say," with a glance full of prognostic complimentary utterances, which a further acquaintance might develop.

As he was lighting the gas of a side bracket that she might better see to read her music, Mrs. Brainard and her daughter came into the room, radiantly attired and both approached Paula with sweet and polite greeting.

"George, in mercy!" exclaimed his mother, "put out that gas, you are killing the effect of the candle light."

"But Miss Von Stoltz can't read her music without it, mother."

"I've no doubt Miss Von Stoltz knows her pieces by heart," Mrs. Brainard replied, seeking corroboration from Paula's glance.

"No, madame; I'm not accustomed to playing dance music, and this is quite new to me," the girl rejoined, touching the loose sheets that George had conveniently straightened out and placed on the rack.

"Oh, dear! 'not accustomed'?" said Miss Brainard. "And Mr. Sohmeir told us he knew you would give satisfaction."

Paula hastened to re-assure the thoroughly alarmed young lady on the point of her ability to give perfect satisfaction.

The door bell now began to ring incessantly. Up the stairs, tripped fleeting opera-cloaked figures, followed by their black robed attendants. The rooms commenced to fill with the pretty hub-bub that a bevy of girls can make when inspired by a close masculine proximity; and Paula, not waiting to be asked, struck the opening bars of an inspiring waltz.

Some hours later, during a lull in the dancing, when the men were making vigorous applications of fans and handkerchiefs; and the girls beginning to throw themselves into attitudes of picturesque exhaustion—save for the always indefatigable few—a proposition was ventured, backed by clamorous entreaties, which induced George to bring forth his banjo. And an agreeable moment followed, in which that young man's skill met with a truly deserving applause. Never had his audience beheld such proficiency as he displayed in the handling of his instrument, which was now behind him, now over-head, and again swinging in mid-air like the pendulum of a clock and sending forth the sounds of stirring melody. Sounds so inspiring that a pretty little black-eyed fairy, an acknowledged votary of Terpsichore, and George's particular admiration, was moved to contribute a few passes of a Virginia break-down, as she had studied it from life on a Southern plantation. The act closing amid a spontaneous babel of hand clapping and admiring bravos.

It must be admitted that this little episode, however graceful, was hardly a fitting prelude to the magnificent "Jewel Song from 'Faust,'" with which Miss Brainard next consented to regale the company. That Miss Brainard possessed a voice, was a fact that had existed as matter of tradition in the family as far back almost as the days of that young lady's baby utterances, in which loving ears had already detected the promise which time had so recklessly fulfilled.

True genius is not to be held in abeyance, though a host of Engfelders would rise to quell it with their mundane protests!

Miss Brainard's rendition was a triumphant achievement of sound, and with the proud flush of success moving her to kind condescension, she asked Miss Von Stoltz to "please play something."

Paula amiably consented, choosing a selection from the Modern Classic. How little did her auditors appreciate in the performance the results of a life study, of a drilling that had made her amongst the knowing an acknowledged mistress of technique. But to her skill she added the touch and interpretation of the artist; and in hearing her, even Ignorance paid to her genius the tribute of a silent emotion.

When she arose there was a moment of quiet, which was broken by the black-eyed fairy, always ready to cast herself into a breach, observing, flippantly, "How pretty!" "Just lovely!" from another; and "What wouldn't I give to play like that." Each inane compliment falling like a dash of cold water on Paula's ardor.

She then became solicitous about the hour, with reference to her car, and George who stood near looked at his watch and informed her that the last car had gone by a full half hour before.

"But," he added, "if you are not expecting any one to call for you, I will gladly see you home."

"I expect no one, for the car that passes here would have set me down at my door," and in this avowal of difficulties, she tacitly accepted George's offer.

The situation was new. It gave her a

feeling of elation to be walking through the quiet night with this handsome young fellow. He talked so freely and so pleasantly. She felt such a comfort in his strong protective nearness. In clinging to him against the buffets of the staggering wind she could feel the muscles of his arms, like steel.

He was so unlike any man of her acquaintance. Strictly unlike Poldorf, the pianist, the short rotundity of whose person could have been less objectionable, if she had not known its cause to lie in an inordinate consumption of beer. Old Engfelder, with his long hair, his spectacles and his loose, disjointed figure, was hors de combat in comparison. And of Max Kuntzler, the talented composer, her teacher of harmony, she could at the moment think of no positive point of objection against him, save the vague, general, serious one of his unlikeness to George.

Her new awakened admiration, though, was not deaf to a little inexplicable wish that he had not been so proficient with the banjo.

On they went chatting gaily, until turning the corner of the street in which she lived, Paula saw that before the door stood Dr. Sinn's buggy.

Brainard could feel the quiver of surprised distress that shook her frame, as she said, hurrying along, "Oh! mamma must be ill—worse; they have called the doctor."

Reaching the house, she threw open wide the door that was unlocked, and he stood hesitatingly back. The gas in the small hall burned at its full, and showed Berta at the top of the stairs, speechless, with terrified eyes, looking down at her. And coming to meet her, was a neighbor, who strove with well-meaning solicitude to keep her back, to hold her yet a moment in ignorance of the cruel blow that fate had dealt her whilst she had in happy unconsciousness played her music for the dance.

III

SEVERAL MONTHS HAD passed since the dreadful night when death had deprived Paula for the second time of a loved parent.

After the first shock of grief was over, the girl had thrown all her energies into work, with the view of attaining that position in the musical world which her father and mother had dreamed might be hers.

She had remained in the small home occupying now but the half of it; and here she kept house with the faithful Berta's aid.

Friends were both kind and attentive to the stricken girl. But there had been two, whose constant devotion spoke of an interest deeper than mere friendly solicitude.

Max Kuntzler's love for Paula was something that had taken hold of his sober middle age with an enduring strength which was not to be lessened or shaken, by her rejection of it. He had asked leave to remain her friend, and while holding the tender, watchful privileges which that comprehensive title may imply, had refrained from further thrusting a warmer feeling on her acceptance.

Paula one evening was seated in her small sitting-room, working over some musical transpositions, when a ring at the bell was followed by a footstep in the hall which made her hand and heart tremble.

George Brainard entered the room, and before she could rise to greet him, had seated himself in the vacant chair beside her.

"What an untiring worker you are," he said, glancing down at the scores before her.

"I always feel that my presence interrupts you; and yet I don't know that a judicious interruption isn't the wholesomest thing for you sometimes."

"You forget," she said, smiling into his face, "that I was trained to it. I must keep myself fitted to my calling. Rest would mean deterioration."

"Would you not be willing to follow some other calling?" he asked, looking at her with unusual earnestness in his dark, handsome eyes.

"Oh, never!"

"Not if it were a calling that asked only for the labor of loving?"

She made no answer, but kept her eyes fixed on the idle traceries that she drew with her pencil on the sheets before her.

He arose and made a few impatient turns about the room, then coming again to her side, said abruptly:

"Paula, I love you. It isn't telling you something that you don't know, unless you have been without bodily perceptions. To-day there is something driving me to speak it out in words. Since I have known you," he continued, striving to look into her face that bent low over the work before her, "I have been mounting into higher and always higher circles of Paradise, under a blessed illusion that you—cared for me. But to-day, a feeling of dread has been forcing itself upon me—dread that with a word you might throw me back into a gulf that would now be one of everlasting misery. Say if you love me, Paula. I believe you do, and yet I wait with indefinable doubts for your answer."

He took her hand which she did not withdraw from his.

"Why are you speechless? Why don't you say something to me!" he asked desperately.

"I am speechless with joy and misery," she answered. "To know that you love me, gives me happiness enough to brighten a lifetime. And I am miserable, feeling that you have spoken the signal that must part us."

"You love me, and speak of parting. Never! You will be my wife. From this moment we belong to each other. Oh, my Paula," he said, drawing her to his side, "my whole existence will be devoted to your happiness."

"I can't marry you," she said shortly, disengaging his hand from her waist.

"Why?" he asked abruptly. They stood looking into each other's eyes.

"Because it doesn't enter into the purpose of my life."

"I don't ask you to give up anything in your life. I only beg you to let me share it with you."

George had known Paula only as the

daughter of the undemonstrative American woman. He had never before seen her with the father's emotional nature aroused in her. The color mounted into her cheeks, and her blue eyes were almost black with intensity of feeling.

"Hush," she said; "don't tempt me further." And she cast herself on her knees before the table near which they stood, gathering the music that lay upon it into an armful, and resting her hot cheek upon it.

"What do you know of my life," she exclaimed passionately. "What can you guess of it? Is music anything more to you than the pleasing distraction of an idle moment? Can't you feel that with me, it courses with the blood through my veins? That it's something dearer than life, than riches, even than love?" with a quiver of pain.

"Paula listen to me; don't speak like a mad woman."

She sprang up and held out an arm to ward away his nearer approach.

"Would you go into a convent, and ask to be your wife a nun who has vowed herself to the service of God?"

"Yes, if that nun loved me; she would owe to herself, to me and to God to be my wife."

Paula seated herself on the sofa, all emotion seeming suddenly to have left her; and he came and sat beside her.

"Say only that you love me, Paula," he urged persistently.

"I love you," she answered low and with pale lips.

He took her in his arms, holding her in silent rapture against his heart and kissing the white lips back into red life.

"You will be my wife?"

"You must wait. Come back in a week and I will answer you." He was forced to be content with the delay.

The days of probation being over, George went for his answer, which was given him by the old lady who occupied the upper story.

"Ach Gott! Fräulein Von Stoltz ist schon im Leipsic gegangen!"—All that has not been many years ago. George Brainard is as handsome as ever, though growing a little stout in the quiet routine of domestic life. He has quite lost a pretty taste for music that formerly distinguished him as a skilful banjoist. This loss his little black-eyed wife deplores; though she has herself made concessions to the advancing years, and abandoned Virginia break-downs as incompatible with the serious offices of wifehood and matrimony.

You may have seen in the morning paper, that the renowned pianist, Fräulein Paula Von Stoltz, is resting in Leipsic, after an extended and remunerative concert tour.

Professor Max Kuntzler is also in Leipsic—with the ever persistent will—the dogged patience that so often wins in the end.

A POINT AT ISSUE!

Married—On Tuesday, May 11, Eleanor Gail to Charles Faraday.

Nothing bearing the shape of a wedding announcement could have been less obtrusive than the foregoing hidden in a remote corner of the Plymdale *Promulgator*, clothed in the palest and smallest of type, and modestly wedged in between the big, black-lettered offer of the *Promulgator* to mail itself free of extra charge to subscribers leaving home for the summer months, and an equally somber-clad notice (doubtless astray as to place and application) that Hammersmith & Co. were carrying a large and varied assortment of marble and granite monuments!

Yet notwithstanding its sandwiched condition, that little marriage announcement seemed to Eleanor to parade the whole street.

Whichever way she turned her eyes, it glowered at her with scornful reproach.

She felt it to be an indelicate thrusting of herself upon the public notice; and at the sight she was plunged in regret at having made to the proprieties the concession of permitting it.

She hoped now that the period for making concessions was ended. She had endured long and patiently the trials that beset her path when she chose to diverge from the beaten walks of female Plymdaledom. Had stood stoically enough the questionable distinction of being relegated to a place amid that large and ill-assorted family of "cranks," feeling the discomfit and attending opprobrium to be far out-balanced by the satisfying consciousness of roaming the heights of free thought, and tasting the sweets of a spiritual emancipation.

The closing act of Eleanor's young ladyhood, when she chose to be married without pre-announcement, without the paraphernalia of accessories so dear to a curious public—had been in keeping with previous methods distinguishing her career. The disappointed public cheated of its entertainment, was forced to seek such compensation for the loss as was offered in reflections that while condemning her present, were unsparing of her past, and full with damning prognostic of her future.

Charles Faraday, who added to his unembellished title that of Professor of

Mathematics of the Plymdale University, had found in Eleanor Gail his ideal woman.

Indeed, she rather surpassed that ideal, which had of necessity been but an adorned picture of woman as he had known her. A mild emphasizing of her merits, a soft toning down of her defects had served to offer to his fancy a prototype of that bequoted creature.

"Not too good for human nature's daily food," yet so good that he had cherished no hope of beholding such a one in the flesh. Until Eleanor had come, supplanting his ideal, and making of that fanciful creation a very simpleton by contrast. In the beginning he had found her extremely good to look at, with her combination of graceful womanly charms, unmarred by self-conscious mannerisms that was as rare as it was engaging. Talking with her, he had caught a look from her eyes into his that he recognized at once as a free masonry of intellect. And the longer he knew her, the greater grew his wonder at the beautiful revelations of her mind that unfurled itself to his, like the curling petals of some hardy blossom that opens to the inviting warmth of the sun. It was not that Eleanor knew many things. According to her own modest estimate of herself, she knew nothing. There were school girls in Plymdale who surpassed her in the amount of their positive knowledge. But she was possessed of a clear intellect: sharp in its reasoning, strong and unprejudiced in its outlook. She was that *rara avis*, a logical woman— something which Faraday had not encountered in his life before. True, he was not hoary with age. At 30 the types of women he had met with were not legion; but he felt safe in doubting that the hedges of the future would grow logical women for him, more than they had borne such prodigies in the past.

He found Eleanor ready to take broad views of life and humanity; able to grasp a question and anticipate conclusions by a quick intuition which he himself reached by the slower, consecutive steps of reason.

During the months that shaped themselves into the cycle of a year these two dwelt together in the harmony of a united purpose.

Together they went looking for the good things of life, knocking at the closed doors of philosophy; venturing into the open fields of science, she, with uncertain steps, made steady by his help.

Whithersoever he led she followed, oftentimes in her eagerness taking the lead into unfamiliar ways in which he, weighted with a lingering conservatism, had hesitated to venture.

So did they grow in their oneness of thought to belong each so absolutely to the other that the idea seemed not to have come to them that this union might be made faster by marriage. Until one day it broke upon Faraday, like a revelation from the unknown, the possibility of making her his wife.

When he spoke, eager with the new awakened impulse, she laughingly replied:

"Why not?" She had thought of it long ago.

In entering upon their new life they decided to be governed by no precedential methods. Marriage was to be a form, that while fixing legally their relation to each other, was in no wise to touch the individuality of either; that was to be preserved intact. Each was to remain a free integral of humanity, responsible to no dominating exactions of so-called marriage laws. And the element that was to make possible such a union was trust in each other's love, honor, courtesy, tempered by the reserving clause of readiness to meet the consequences of reciprocal liberty.

Faraday appreciated the need of offering to his wife advantages for culture which had been of impossible attainment during her girlhood.

Marriage, which marks too often the closing period of a woman's intellectual existence, was to be in her case the open portal through which she might seek the embellishments that her strong, graceful mentality deserved.

An urgent desire with Eleanor was to acquire a thorough speaking knowledge of the French language. They agreed that a lengthy sojourn in Paris could be the only practical and reliable means of accomplishing such an end.

Faraday's three months of vacation were

to be spent by them in the idle happiness of a loitering honeymoon through the continent of Europe, then he would leave his wife in the French capital for a stay that might extend indefinitely—two, three years—as long as should be found needful, he returning to join her with the advent of each summer, to renew their love in a fresh and re-strengthened union.

And so, in May, they were married, and in September we find Eleanor established in the pension of the old couple Clairegobeau and comfortably ensconced in her pretty room that opened on to the Rue Rivoli, her heart full of sweet memories that were to cheer her coming solitude.

On the wall, looking always down at her with his quiet, kind glance, hung the portrait of her husband. Beneath it stood the fanciful little desk at which she hoped to spend many happy hours.

Books were everywhere, giving character to the graceful furnishings which their united taste had evolved from the paucity of the Clairegobeau germ, and out of the window was Paris!

Eleanor was supremely satisfied amid her new and attractive surroundings. The pang of parting from her husband seeming to lend sharp zest to a situation that offered the fulfillment of a cherished purpose.

Faraday, with the stronger man-nature, felt more keenly the discomfit of giving up a companionship that in its brief duration had been replete with the duality of accomplished delight and growing promise.

But to him also was the situation made acceptable by its involving a principle which he felt it incumbent upon him to uphold. He returned to Plymdale and to his duties at the university, and resumed his bachelor existence as quietly as though it had been interrupted but by the interval of a day.

The small public with which he had acquaintance, and which had forgotten his existence during the past few months, was fired anew with indignant astonishment at the effrontery of the situation which his singular coming back offered to their contemplation.

That two young people should presume to introduce such innovations into matrimony!

It was uncalled for!

It was improper!

It was indecent!

He must have already tired of her idiosyncrasies, since he had left her in Paris.

And in Paris, of all places, to leave a young woman alone! Why not at once in Hades?

She had been left in Paris forsooth

to learn French. And since when was Mme. Belaire's French, as it had been taught to select generations of Plymdalions, considered insufficient for the practical needs of existence as related by that foreign tongue?

But Faraday's life was full with occupation and his brief moments of leisure were too precious to give to heeding the idle gossip that floated to his hearing and away again without holding his thoughts an instant.

He lived uninterruptedly a certain existence with his wife through the medium of letters. True, an inadequate substitute for her actual presence, but there was much satisfaction in this constant communion of thought between them.

They told such details of their daily lives as they thought worth the telling.

Their readings were discussed. Opinions exchanged. Newspaper cuttings sent back and forth, bearing upon questions that interested them. And what did not interest them?

Nothing was so large that they dared not look at it. Happenings, small in themselves, but big in their psychological comprehensiveness, held them with strange fascination. Her earnestness and intensity in such matters were extreme; but happily, Faraday brought to this union humorous instincts, and an optimism that saved it from a too monotonous sombreness.

The young man had his friends in Plymdale. Certainly none that ever remotely approached the position which Eleanor held in that regard. She stood pre-eminent. She was himself.

But his nature was genial. He invited companionship from his fellow beings, who, however short that companionship might be, carried always away a gratifying

consciousness of having made their person-
alities felt.

The society in Plymdale which he most
frequented was that of the Beatons.

Beaton père was a fellow professor,
many years older than Faraday, but one of
those men with whom time, after putting its
customary stamp upon his outward being,
took no further care.

The spirit of his youth had remained
untouched, and formed the nucleus around
which the family gathered, drawing the
light of their own cheerfulness.

Mrs. Beaton was a woman whose as-
pirations went not further than the desire
for her family's good, and her bearing announced in its every feature, the satisfaction
of completed hopes.

Of the daughters, Margaret, the eld-
est, was looked upon as slightly erratic,

owing to a timid leaning in the direction of Woman's Suffrage.

Her activity in that regard, taking the form of a desultory correspondence with members of a certain society of protest; the fashioning and donning of garments of mysterious shape, which, while stamping their wearer with the distinction of a quasi-emancipation, defeated the ultimate purpose of their construction by inflicting a personal discomfort that extended beyond the powers of long endurance. Miss Kitty Beaton, the youngest daughter, and just returned from boarding-school, while clamoring for no privileges doubtful of attainment and of remote and questionable benefit, with a Napoleonic grip, possessed herself of such rights as were at hand and exercised them in keeping the household under her capricious command.

She was at that age of blissful illusion when a girl is in love with her own youth and beauty and happiness. That age which heeds no purpose in the scope of creation further than may touch her majesty's enjoyment. Who would not smilingly endure with that charming selfishness of youth, knowing that the rough hand of experience is inevitably descending to disturb the short-lived dream?

They were all clever people, bright and interesting, and in this family circle Faraday found an acceptable relaxation from work and enforced solitude.

If they ever doubted the wisdom or expediency of his domestic relations, courtesy withheld the expression of any such doubts. Their welcome was always complete in its friendliness, and the interest which they evinced in the absent Eleanor proved that she was held in the highest esteem.

With Beaton Faraday enjoyed that pleasant intercourse which may exist between men whose ways, while not too divergent, are yet divided by an appreciable interval.

But it remained for Kitty to touch him with her girlish charms in a way, which, though not too usual with Faraday, meant so little to the man that he did not take the trouble to resent it.

Her laughter and song, the restless motions of her bubbling happiness, he watched with the casual pleasure that one follows the playful gambols of a graceful kitten.

He liked the soft shining light of her eyes. When she was near him the velvet smoothness of her pink cheeks stirred him with a feeling that could have found satisfying expression in a kiss.

It is idle to suppose that even the most exemplary men go through life with their eyes closed to woman's beauty and their senses steeled against its charm.

Faraday thought little of this feeling (and so should we if it were not outspoken).

In writing one day to his wife, with the cold-blooded impartiality of choosing a subject which he thought of neither more nor less prominence than the next, he descanted at some length upon the interesting emotions which Miss Kitty's pretty femininity aroused in him.

If he had given serious thought to the expediency of touching upon such a theme with one's wife, he still would not have been deterred. Was not Eleanor's large comprehensiveness far above the littleness of ordinary women?

Did it not enter into the scheme of their lives, to keep free from prejudices that hold their sway over the masses?

But he thought not of that, for, after all,

his interest in Kitty and his interest in his university class bore about an equal reference to Eleanor and his love for her.

His letter was sent, and he gave no second thought to the matter of its contents.

The months went by for Faraday with few distinctive features to mark them outside the enduring desire for his wife's presence.

There had been a visit of sharp disturbance once when her customary letter failed him, and the tardy missive coming, carried an inexplicable coldness that dealt him a pain which, however, did not long survive a little judicious reflection and a very deluge of letters from Paris that shook him with their unusual ardor.

May had come again, and at its approach Faraday with the impatience of a hundred lovers hastened across the seas to join his Eleanor.

It was evening and Eleanor paced to and fro in her room, making the last of a series of efforts that she had been putting forth all day to fight down a misery of the heart, against which her reason was in armed rebellion. She had tried the strategy of simply ignoring its presence, but the attempt had failed utterly. During her daily walk it had embodied itself in every object that her eyes rested upon. It had enveloped her like a smoke mist, through which Paris looked more dull than the desolation of Sahara.

She had thought to displace it with work, but, like the disturbing element in the chemist's crucible, it rose again and again overspreading the surface of her labor.

Alone in her room, the hour had come when she meant to succeed by the unaided force of reason—proceeding first to make herself bodily comfortable in the folds of a majestic flowing gown, in which she looked a distressed goddess.

Her hair hung heavy and free about her shoulders, for those reasoning powers were to be spurred by a plunging of white fingers into the golden mass.

In this dishevelled state Eleanor's presence seemed too large for the room and its delicate furnishings. The place fitted well an Eleanor in repose but not an Eleanor who swept the narrow confines like an incipient cyclone.

Reason did good work and stood its ground bravely, but against it were the too great odds of a woman's heart, backed by the soft prejudices of a far-reaching heredity.

She finally sank into a chair before her pretty writing desk. The golden head fell upon the outspread arms waiting to receive it, and she burst into a storm of sobs and tears. It was the signal of surrender.

It is a gratifying privilege to be permitted to ignore the reason of such unusual disturbance in a woman of Eleanor's high qualifications. The cause of that abandonment of grief will never be learned unless she chooses to disclose it herself.

When Faraday first folded his wife in his arms he saw but the Eleanor of his constant dreams. But he soon began to perceive how more beautiful she had grown; with a richness of coloring and fullness of health that Plymdale had never been able to bestow. And the object of her stay in Paris was gaining fast to accomplishment, for she had already acquired a knowledge of French that would not require much longer to perfect.

They sat together in her room discussing plans for the summer, when a timid knock at the door caused Eleanor to look up, to see the little housemaid eyeing her with the glance of a fellow conspirator and holding in her hand a card that she suffered to be but partly visible.

Eleanor hastily approached her, and reading the name upon the card thrust it into her pocket, exchanging some whispered words with the girl, among which were audible, "excuse me," "engaged," "another time." She came back to her husband looking a little flustered, to resume the conversation where it had been interrupted and he offered no inquiries about her mysterious caller.

Entering the salon not many days later he found that in doing so he interrupted a conversation between his wife and a very striking looking gentleman who seemed on the point of taking his leave.

They were both disconcerted; she especially, in bowing, almost thrusting him out, had the appearance of wanting to run away; to do any thing but meet her husband's glance.

He asked with assumed indifference who her friend might be. "Oh, no one special," with a hopeless attempt at brazenness. He accepted the situation without protest, only indulging the reflection that Eleanor was losing something of her frankness.

But when his wife asked him on another occasion to dispense with her company for a whole afternoon, saying that she had an urgent call upon her time, he began to wonder if there might not be modifications to this marital liberty of which he was so staunch an advocate.

She left him with a hundred little endearments that she seemed to have acquired with her French.

He forced himself to the writing of a few urgent letters, but his restlessness did not permit him to do more.

It drove him to ugly thoughts, then to the means of dispelling them.

He gazed out of the window, wondered why he was remaining indoors, and followed up the reflection by seizing his hat and plunging out into the street.

The Paris boulevards of a day in early summer are calculated to dispel almost any ache but one of that nature, which was making itself incipiently felt with Faraday.

It was at that stage when it moves a man to take exception at the inadequacy of every thing that is offered to his contemplation or entertainment.

The sun was too hot.

The shop windows were vulgar; lacking artistic detail in their make-up.

How could he ever have found the Paris women attractive? They had lost their chic. Most of them were scrawny—not worth looking at.

He thought to go and stroll through the galleries of art. He knew Eleanor would wish to be with him; then he was tempted to go alone.

Finally, more tired from inward than outward restlessness, he took refuge at one of the small tables of a café, called for a "Mazarin," and, so seated for an unheeded time, let the panorama of Paris pass before his indifferent eyes.

When suddenly one of the scenes in this shifting show struck him with stunning effect.

It was the sight of his wife riding in a fiacre with her caller of a few days back, both conversing and in high spirits.

He remained for a moment enervated, then the blood came tingling back into his veins like fire, making his finger ends twitch with a desire (full worthy of any one of the "prejudiced masses") to tear the scoundrel from his seat and paint the boulevard red with his villainous blood.

A rush of wild intentions crowded into his brain.

Should he follow and demand an explanation? Leave Paris without ever looking into her face again? and more not worthy of the man.

It is right to say that his better self and better senses came quickly back to him.

That first revolt was like the unwilling protest of the flesh against the surgeon's knife before a man has steeled himself to its endurance.

Every thing came back to him from their short, common past—their dreams, their large intentions for the shaping of their lives. Here was the first test, and should he be the one to cry out, "I cannot endure it."

When he returned to the pension, Eleanor was impatiently waiting for him in the entry, radiant with gladness at his coming.

She was under a suppressed excitement

that prevented her noting his disturbed appearance.

She took his listless hand and led him into the small drawing-room that adjoined their sleeping chamber.

There stood her companion of the fiacre, smiling as was she at the pleasure of introducing him to another Eleanor disposed on the wall in the best possible light to display the gorgeous radiance of her wonderful beauty and the skill of the man who had portrayed it.

The most sanguine hopes of Eleanor and her artist could not have anticipated anything like the rapture with which Faraday received this surprise.

"Monsieur l'Artiste" went away with his belief in the undemonstrativeness of the American very much shaken; and in his pocket substantial evidence of American appreciation of art.

Then the story was told how the portrait was intended as a surprise for his arrival. How there had been delay in its completion. The artist had required one more sitting, which she gave him that day, and the two had brought the picture home in the fiacre, he to give it the final advantages of a judicious light; to witness its effect upon Mons. Faraday and finally the excusable wish to be presented to the husband of the lady who had captivated his deepest admiration and esteem.

"You shall take it home with you," said Eleanor.

Both were looking at the lovely creation by the soft light of a reckless expenditure of bougie.

"Yes, dearest," he answered, with feeble elation at the prospect of returning home with that exquisite piece of inanimation.

"Have you engaged your return passage?" she asked.

She sat at his knee, arrayed in the gown that had one evening clothed such a goddess in distress.

"Oh, no. There's plenty time for that," was his answer. "Why do you ask?"

"I'm sure I don't know," and after a while:

"Charlie, I think—I mean, don't you think—I have made wonderful progress in French?"

"You've done marvels, Nellie. I find no difference between your French and Mme. Clairegobeau's, except that yours is far prettier."

"Yes?" she rejoined, with a little squeeze of the hand.

"I mayn't be right and I want you to give me your candid opinion. I believe Mme. Belaire—now that I have gone so far—don't you think—hadn't you better engage passage for two?"

His answer took the form of a panto-mimic rapture of assenting gratefulness, during which each gave speechless assur-ance of a love that could never more take a second place.

"Nellie," he asked, looking into the face that nestled in close reach of his warm kisses, "I have often wanted to know, though you needn't tell it if it doesn't suit you," he added, laughing, "why you once failed to write to me, and then sent a let-ter whose coldness gave me a week's heart trouble?"

She flushed, and hesitated, but finally answered him bravely, "It was when—when you cared so much for that Kitty Beaton."

Astonishment for a moment deprived him of speech.

"But Eleanor! In the name of reason! It isn't possible!"

"I know all you would say," she replied,

"I have been over the whole ground myself, over and over, but it is useless. I have found that there are certain things which a woman can't philosophize about, any more than she can about death when it touches that which is near to her."

"But you don't think—"

"Hush! don't speak of it ever again. I think nothing!" closing her eyes, and with a little shudder drawing closer to him.

As he kissed his wife with passionate fondness, Faraday thought, "I love her none the less for it, but my Nellie is only a woman, after all."

With man's usual inconsistency, he had quite forgotten the episode of the portrait.

MRS. MOBRY'S
REASON

It was in the springtime and under the blossom-laden branches of an apple tree that Editha Payne finally accepted John Mobry for her husband.

For three years she had been refusing him, with an obstinacy that made people wonder only a little less than they marvelled at the persistence of his desire to marry her. She was simply a nobody—an English girl with antecedents shrouded in obscurity; a governess, moreover; not in her first youth, and none too handsome. But John Mobry was of that class of men who, when they want something, usually keep on wanting it and striving for it so long as there is possibility of attainment in view.

Chance brought him to her that spring day out under the blossoms, at a moment when inward forces were at work with her to weaken and undo the determination of a lifetime.

She looked away from him, far away across the green hills that the sun had touched and quickened, and beyond, into the impenetrable mist. Her tired face wore the look of the conquered who has made a brave fight and would rest.

"Well, John, if you want it," she said, placing her hand in his.

And as she did so she formed the inward resolve that her eyes should never again look into the impenetrable mist. But why she had ever rejected him was something which people kept on asking themselves and each other for the length of time that people will ask such things.

The answer came slowly—twenty-five years later. Most people had forgotten by that time that they ever wanted to know why.

II

AGAIN IT WAS springtime.

A young man who had been trying to read, where he lounged in the deep embrasure of a window, turned to say to the girl who sat playing at the piano:

"Naomi, why is it the spring always comes like a revelation—a delicious surprise?"

"Wait, Sigmund," and she played the closing bars of the piece of music that was open before her, then rising, went to join him at the window.

She was a splendid type of physical health and beauty, lithe, supple, firm of flesh, wearing youth's colors in cheek and lip; youth's gloss and glow in the waves of her thick brown hair. Her brown eyes drowsed and gleamed alternately, and questioned often.

"The spring?" she said, "why does it come like a revelation? How should I know? This is surely reversing roles when you question."

She took the book from his hand to glance carelessly through its pages.

"Do you know, you are a very curious young woman," he said, looking at her with something of admiration, but yet superciliously, for he was young, and a college student. "You gave me the same reply this morning when I asked you—what was it, now, I asked you?"

"To define the quality in Chopin's music that charms me. Well," she continued, "I don't know the 'why' of things. That certain sounds, scenes, impressions move me I know, because I feel it. I don't bother about reasons. Remember, Sigmund, I know so little."

"Oh, you want training, no doubt, and it's an immense pity you've never received it. Let us go through a course together this summer. Do you agree to it?"

He was the lordly collegiate, sure of his weapons.

"I don't believe I do, Sigmund," Naomi laughed. "And if I did it would be useless, for mamma never would consent. You know what she thinks of ologies and isms and all that for women."

"Oh, isms and ologies do not constitute solely the training I have in mind."

"Why, my recollection never goes back to any time when books formed an important feature of my life," she interrupted. "I've lived more than half my days under the sky, galloping over the hills, as often as not with the rain stinging my face. Oh, the open air and all that it teems with! There's nothing like it, Sigmund. What color! Look, now, at the purple wrapping those hills away to the east. See the hundred shades of green spreading before us, with the new-plowed fields between making brown dashes and patches. And then the sky, so blue where it frames those white velvet clouds. They'll be red and gold this evening."

"What a greedy eye you have—a veritable savage eye for pure color. Do you know how to use it? to make it serve you?"

"Oh, no, Sigmund," she said. "Music's

the only thing I've studied and learned. Mamma couldn't have prevented that if she'd wanted to, I believe. There's nothing that has the meaning for me in this world that sound has. I feel as if the Truth were going to come to me, some day, through the harmony of it. I wonder if anyone else has an ear so tuned and sharpened as I have, to detect the music, not of the spheres, but of earth, subtleties of major and minor chord that the wind strikes upon the tree branches. Have you ever heard the earth breathe, Sigmund?" she asked, with wide eyes that filled with merriment when she saw the astonishment in his.

Then, half laughing, half singing the gay refrain of a comic opera air, she sprang with quick cat-like movement to her feet, and seizing a foil from against the wall, whirled with it into position in the centre of the room.

Her companion had been as quick to follow. They measured their distances with stately grace, and looked a continuous challenge into each other's eyes. Then for five long minutes, as they stood face to face exchanging skillful thrust and parry, no sound was heard but the clink and scrape of the slender steels; on the hard-wood floor the stamp of advancing feet in the charge. It was only when Mrs. Mobry's long, pale face looked in at the cautiously opened door that the engagement ended.

"Why, Naomi," she said, a little apologetically, coming into the room, "I didn't hear the piano and—"

"And you wondered what disaster could have happened," the girl replied, flushed and amused as she replaced her weapon upon the wall. "I was only giving Cousin Sigmund a lesson with the foils, mamma."

"You know your father comes on the

early train to-day, Naomi; he'll be disappointed if you're not at the station to meet
him, dear."

"And a perfect right he'd have to be disappointed, and bewildered, too. When have
I ever failed him?"

And she quitted the room, making, as
she left it, a pass at Sigmund with an imaginary weapon, and laughing gaily as she
did so.

Mrs. Mobry went to the piano and
gathered together the sheets of music that
Naomi had left there in some disorder, and
arranged them upon the stand. She had the
appearance of seeking occupation; a house
full of servants left her little or none of a
manual sort; for wealth was one of the
things which John Mobry had persistently
wanted, long ago.

Mrs. Mobry was past fifty, with her
hair, that was turning gray, carefully parted

and brushed smooth down upon her temples. When she seated herself and began to rock gently, she drew the cape which she wore closely about her thin shoulders.

"Don't you find it chill, Sigmund," she said, "with that window open? I dare say not, though; young blood is warm."

But Sigmund went and closed the window, making no boast that his veins were scintillant. He only said:

"You're right, Aunt Editha; this early spring air is treacherous."

"I wanted to speak with you a moment alone, dear," she commenced at once, coughing uneasily behind her hand. "It may be, and I trust it is, wholly unnecessary, this caution; but it's best to be open, so far as we can be, in this world. And, of course, when young people are thrown together—"

Sigmund, to quote his thoughts, literally, wondered what his aunt was driving at.

"I only want to say—as you perhaps are not aware of it—that it's our intention, and Naomi's, too, that she shall never marry. As you will be with us all summer I thought it best to acquaint you at once with such little family arrangements, so that we may all feel comfortable and avoid unpleasant consequences." Mrs. Mobry smiled feebly as she said this, and smoothed down the hair on her temples with her long thin hands.

"Has Naomi made you such a promise?" Sigmund asked, thinking it a great pity if she had.

"Oh, there's been no promise, but it has been always understood. I've impressed upon her since she was a little child that she is to remain with me always. It looks selfish—I know it looks selfish; your Uncle John even thinks so, though he has never opposed my wish."

"I see rather a natural instinct in this

wish of yours than cold selfishness, Aunt Editha. Something you can't overcome, perhaps. I remember now hearing how fearfully cut up you were two years ago when Edward married."

Mrs. Mobry grew a shade paler, and her voice trembled when she said:

"I can't pardon Edward. It was treacherous, marrying in that way, knowing how I opposed it. It was unfortunate that your uncle should have sent him to take charge of the business in Middleburg. That marriage could not have come about if he had been here at my side, where his place was."

"But, Aunt Editha, it isn't such a calamity after all. He has married a charming woman, and seems perfectly happy. If you would consent to visit him, and were to see his content with your bodily eyes I think you would be reconciled to his coup d'état."

Sigmund thought his aunt Editha rather

stupidly set in her ideas. But as he had already recognized the possibility of falling in love with his cousin, Naomi, he was not ill-pleased that Mrs. Mobry had so considerately warned him. If he walked into the fire now it would be with open eyes.

Sigmund was the son of Mr. Mobry's sister; a student of medicine, twenty-two years of age, a little run down and overworked, and hoping for recuperation amid these Western hills. He had visited his uncle's family often as a child, when he and his cousin Edward—two years his senior—had been friends. But his absence this time had lasted four years. He had left Naomi an awkward, boisterous girl of fourteen. When he returned he found that she had undergone a seeming re-creation.

He himself was a good-looking young blond fellow, full of hope and belief in his future; though he tried hard to cultivate an interesting cynicism, which he could never succeed in making anyone believe in.

III

HAD MRS. MOBRY'S intention been that Sigmund should fall in love with her daughter she could not have designed a plan more Machiavellian than the one she employed. But her only thought had been a caution against marriage. Thus there was no cause to grumble, for she had done her work well and surely.

This caution served Sigmund as his only shield—poor fool; all others he set aside at once. It was more than a shield. It was a license, drawn, signed, stamped and delivered to his conscience, which permitted him to live at Naomi's side with his young nature all unbridled to wound itself, after the manner of young unbridled natures.

They lived such a joyous life during those spring and summer days, and did so many things that were delightful! For must it not have been a delight to rise when the morning was yet gray, and to tramp— high-booted both of them—through the brush of the hillside, crisp and silvered with dew? To silently wait with ready rifle for the young covey to start with sudden whirr from the fence corners? To watch the east begin to fire and set the wet earth sparkling?

But perhaps they liked it better, or certainly as well, when they sat side by side in Naomi's wagonette and went jogging to town, three miles away, behind the fat, lazy pony who always wanted to stop and drink when they crossed the shallow ford of the Meramec, where the water ran like liquid crystal over the shining pebbles beneath. He always wanted to stop, too, and rest under the branches of the big walnut tree that marked the limit of the Mobrys' field. It was a whim of Naomi's to let her pony do what he wanted to, and as often as not he wanted to nibble the grass that grew tender along the edges of the road.

It is no wonder then that their little jogs to town consumed an incredible length of time. Yet what had they to do with time but to waste it? And this they did from morning till night. Sometimes upon the river that twines like a silver ribbon through the green slopes of Southern Missouri, seated in Naomi's slender boat, they floated in mid-stream when the stars or moon were over them. They skirted the banks, gliding under the shade of hanging willows when the sun grew hot and lurid, as it did often when the summer days came.

Then Sigmund's blue eyes saw nothing in all the world so good to look upon as Naomi's brown ones, that filled with wonder at the sweet trouble which stirred her when she caught his gaze and answered it.

There was much reading in books, too, during that summer time. There are many things in books beside isms and ologies. The world has always its poets who sing. And, strangely enough, Sigmund could think of no training so fit for Naomi's untrammelled thought as to follow Lancelot in his loves or Juliet in her hot despair. And Naomi often sighed over such tales, and wept sometimes, for Sigmund told them from his heart, and they seemed very real.

Mrs. Mobry's first care—and John Mobry's, too, for that matter—was always Naomi's health; then, Naomi's happiness. These had been from babyhood so fixed and well established that the mother could surely have been forgiven had she permitted her solicitude to wane sometimes. But this she never did. The color must be always there in Naomi's cheek, or she must know why it was not. When the girl grew languid and dreamy—the summer being hot—the mother must know why it was so.

"I'm sure I don't know, mamma. This heavy heat would make anyone's blood run a little sluggishly, I think."

IV

ONE MORNING WHEN the family arose and assembled at an early breakfast, it was to find that Naomi had been up long before and had gone for one of her tramps. The gardener had seen her pass when he left his cottage just at daybreak, and she had called to him: "We are no sluggards to lie abed,

Heinrich, when the earth has waked up," so he said.

They thought at every moment she would enter, flushed and dishevelled, to take her place at table. Sigmund was restless because she was not there; Mrs. Mobry anxious, as she gazed constantly from the window and listened to every sound. When the meal ended, and John Mobry was forced to leave for the station without giving Naomi the accustomed morning farewell, it was plainly a thing that gave him annoyance and pain, for that early kiss from the daughter he loved was a day's inspiration to him.

Sigmund went in search of her. He was quite sure she would be up on the summit of that nearest hill, seated upon the rocky plateau that he knew. But she was not there, nor in the oak grove, nor in any of the places where he looked. The time was speeding, and the sun had grown fierce. He retraced his steps, sure that he would find her at home when he reached there. Passing an opening in the wood that led down to the river, and where it was narrow, he turned instinctively, thinking that she might be there by the water, where she loved to sit. And there he found her. But she was across the stream in her boat, resting motionless under the willow branches, her big straw hat hanging down over the side of her face.

"Naomi! oh, Naomi!" Sigmund called.

At the sound of his voice she looked up, then seizing the oars she pulled with vigorous strokes across the water toward the spot where he stood waiting for her. She sprang from the boat, heedless of the aid which he offered, and passing him quickly, hastened up the slope, where she seated herself, when she had reached its summit, upon the huge trunk of a fallen tree.

Sigmund followed in some surprise, and went to sit beside her.

"We mustn't linger here too long, Naomi; Aunt Editha is worried about your absence. Why did you stay so long away? You shouldn't do such cruel things."

"Sigmund," she whispered, and drawing nearer to him twined her arms around his neck. "I want you to kiss me, Sigmund."

Had the earth trembled, that Sigmund shook like that? And had the sky and the air grown red before his eyes? Were his arms turned wooden that they should hang at his side, when hers were around him? He was hoping a senseless hope for strength when she kissed him. Then his arms did their office. He could not help it; he was young and so human. But he sought no further kiss. He only sat motionless with Naomi in his arms; her head resting upon his heart where his pulses had gone mad.

"Ah, Sigmund, this is just as I was dreaming it this morning when I awoke. Then I was angry because you were sleeping off there in your room like a senseless log, when I was awake and wanted you. And you slept on and never came to me. How could you do it? I was angry and went away and walked over the hills. I thought you would come after me, but you never did. I wouldn't go back till you came. And just now, I went in the boat, and when I was out there in the middle of the stream—listen, Sigmund—the sun struck me upon the head, with something in its hand—no, no, not in his hand—"

"Naomi!"

"And after that I didn't care, for I know everything now. I know what the birds are saying up in the trees—"

"Naomi, look at me!"

"Like Siegfried when he played upon

his pipe under a tree, last winter in town. I can tell you everything that the fishes say in the water. They were talking under the boat when you called me—"

"Naomi! Oh, God—Naomi, look at me!"

He did look into her eyes then—her eyes that he loved so, and there was no more light in them.

"Aunt Editha," said Sigmund, entering his aunt's room, where she was in restless movement, as she had been all morning— "Aunt Editha, Naomi is in the library. I left her there. She must have been chilled by the early morning air, I'm afraid. And the sun seems to have made her ill—wait—Aunt Editha—," for Mrs. Mobry had clutched Sigmund's arm with fingers like steel, and was staggering toward the library.

"How dare you tell me Naomi's ill? She can't be ill," she gasped; "she was never ill in all her life."

They had reached the library, and facing the door through which they entered Naomi sat upon a lounge. She was playing like a little child, with scraps of paper that she was tearing and placing in rows upon the cushion beside her. An instant more, and Mrs. Mobry lay in Sigmund's arms like one dead.

But when night came she kneeled, sobbing as a culprit might, at her husband's feet, telling him a broken story that he scarcely heeded in his anguish.

"It has been in the blood that is mine for generations, John, and I knew it, and I married you.

"Oh, God! if it might end with me and with her—my stricken dove! But, John," she whispered with a new terror in her eyes,

"Edward has already a child. Others will be born to him, and I see the crime of my marriage reaching out to curse me through the lips of generations that will come."

THE STORY OF
AN HOUR

Knowing that Mrs. Mallard was afflicted with a heart trouble, great care was taken to break to her as gently as possible the news of her husband's death.

It was her sister Josephine who told her, in broken sentences; veiled hints that revealed in half concealing. Her husband's friend Richards was there, too, near her. It was he who had been in the newspaper office when intelligence of the railroad disaster was received, with Brently Mallard's name leading the list of "killed." He had only taken the time to assure himself of its truth by a second telegram, and had hastened to forestall any less careful, less tender friend in bearing the sad message.

She did not hear the story as many women have heard the same, with a paralyzed inability to accept its significance. She wept at once, with sudden, wild abandonment, in her sister's arms. When the storm of grief had spent itself she went away to her room alone. She would have no one follow her.

There stood, facing the open window, a comfortable, roomy armchair. Into this she sank, pressed down by a physical exhaustion that haunted her body and seemed to reach into her soul.

She could see in the open square before her house the tops of trees that were all aquiver with the new spring life. The delicious breath of rain was in the air. In the street below a peddler was crying his wares. The notes of a distant song which some one was singing reached her faintly, and countless sparrows were twittering in the eaves.

There were patches of blue sky showing here and there through the clouds that had met and piled one above the other in the west facing her window.

She sat with her head thrown back upon the cushion of the chair, quite motionless, except when a sob came up into her throat and shook her, as a child who has cried itself to sleep continues to sob in its dreams.

She was young, with a fair, calm face, whose lines bespoke repression and even a certain strength. But now there was a dull stare in her eyes, whose gaze was fixed away off yonder on one of those patches of blue sky. It was not a glance of reflection, but rather indicated a suspension of intelligent thought.

There was something coming to her and she was waiting for it, fearfully. What was it? She did not know; it was too subtle and elusive to name. But she felt it, creeping out of the sky, reaching toward her through the sounds, the scents, the color that filled the air.

Now her bosom rose and fell tumultuously. She was beginning to recognize this thing that was approaching to possess her, and she was striving to beat it back with her will—as powerless as her two white slender hands would have been.

When she abandoned herself a little whispered word escaped her slightly parted lips. She said it over and over under her breath: "free, free, free!" The vacant stare and the look of terror that had followed it went from her eyes. They stayed keen and bright. Her pulses beat fast, and the coursing blood warmed and relaxed every inch of her body.

She did not stop to ask if it were or were not a monstrous joy that held her. A clear and exalted perception enabled her to dismiss the suggestion as trivial.

She knew that she would weep again when she saw the kind, tender hands folded in death; the face that had never looked save with love upon her, fixed and gray and dead. But she saw beyond that bitter moment a long procession of years to come that would belong to her absolutely. And she opened and spread her arms out to them in welcome.

There would be no one to live for her during those coming years; she would live for herself. There would be no powerful will bending hers in that blind persistence with which men and women believe they have a right to impose a private will upon a fellow-creature. A kind intention or a cruel intention made the act seem no less a crime as she looked upon it in that brief moment of illumination.

And yet she had loved him—sometimes. Often she had not. What did it matter! What could love, the unsolved mystery, count for in face of this possession of self-assertion which she suddenly recognized as the strongest impulse of her being!

"Free! Body and soul free!" she kept whispering.

Josephine was kneeling before the closed door with her lips to the keyhole, imploring for admission. "Louise, open the door! I beg; open the door—you will make yourself ill. What are you doing, Louise? For heaven's sake open the door."

"Go away. I am not making myself ill." No; she was drinking in a very elixir of life through that open window.

Her fancy was running riot along those

days ahead of her. Spring days, and summer days, and all sorts of days that would be her own. She breathed a quick prayer that life might be long. It was only yesterday she had thought with a shudder that life might be long.

She arose at length and opened the door to her sister's importunities. There was a feverish triumph in her eyes, and she carried herself unwittingly like a goddess of Victory. She clasped her sister's waist, and together they descended the stairs. Richards stood waiting for them at the bottom.

Some one was opening the front door with a latchkey. It was Brently Mallard who entered, a little travel-stained, composedly carrying his grip-sack and umbrella. He had been far from the scene of accident, and did not even know there had been one. He stood amazed at Josephine's piercing cry; at

Richards' quick motion to screen him from the view of his wife.

But Richards was too late.

When the doctors came they said she had died of heart disease—of joy that kills.

A PAIR OF SILK
STOCKINGS

L ittle Mrs. Sommers one day found herself the unexpected possessor of fifteen
dollars. It seemed to her a very large amount
of money, and the way in which it stuffed
and bulged her worn old *porte-monnaie*
gave her a feeling of importance such as she
had not enjoyed for years.

The question of investment was one
that occupied her greatly. For a day or two
she walked about apparently in a dreamy
state, but really absorbed in speculation and
calculation. She did not wish to act hastily,

to do anything she might afterward regret. But it was during the still hours of the night when she lay awake revolving plans in her mind that she seemed to see her way clearly toward a proper and judicious use of the money.

A dollar or two should be added to the price usually paid for Janie's shoes, which would insure their lasting an appreciable time longer than they usually did. She would buy so and so many yards of percale for new shirt waists for the boys and Janie and Mag. She had intended to make the old ones do by skilful patching. Mag should have another gown. She had seen some beautiful patterns, veritable bargains in the shop windows. And still there would be left enough for new stockings—two pairs apiece—and what darning that would save for a while! She would get caps for the boys and sailor-hats for the girls. The vision of her little brood looking fresh and dainty and new for once in their lives excited her and made her restless and wakeful with anticipation.

The neighbors sometimes talked of certain "better days" that little Mrs. Sommers had known before she had ever thought of being Mrs. Sommers. She herself indulged in no such morbid retrospection. She had no time—no second of time to devote to the past. The needs of the present absorbed her every faculty. A vision of the future like some dim, gaunt monster sometimes appalled her, but luckily to-morrow never comes.

Mrs. Sommers was one who knew the value of bargains; who could stand for hours making her way inch by inch toward the desired object that was selling below cost. She could elbow her way if need be; she had learned to clutch a piece of goods and hold it and stick to it with persistence and determination till her turn came to be served, no matter when it came.

But that day she was a little faint and tired. She had swallowed a light luncheon— no! when she came to think of it, between getting the children fed and the place righted, and preparing herself for the shopping bout, she had actually forgotten to eat any luncheon at all!

She sat herself upon a revolving stool before a counter that was comparatively deserted, trying to gather strength and courage to charge through an eager multitude that was besieging breast-works of shirting and figured lawn. An all-gone limp feeling had come over her and she rested her hand aimlessly upon the counter. She wore no gloves. By degrees she grew aware that her hand had encountered something very soothing, very pleasant to touch. She looked down to see that her hand lay upon a pile of silk stockings. A placard near by announced that they had been reduced in price from two dollars and fifty cents to one dollar and ninety-eight cents; and a young girl who stood behind the counter asked her if she wished to examine their line of silk hosiery. She smiled, just as if she had been asked to inspect a tiara of diamonds with the ultimate view of purchasing it. But she went on feeling the soft, sheeny luxurious things—with both hands now, holding them up to see them glisten, and to feel them glide serpent-like through her fingers.

Two hectic blotches came suddenly into her pale cheeks. She looked up at the girl.

"Do you think there are any eights-and-a-half among these?"

There were any number of eights-and-a-half. In fact, there were more of that size than any other. Here was a light-blue pair; there were some lavender, some all black and various shades of tan and gray. Mrs. Sommers selected a black pair and looked at them very long and closely. She pretended to be examining their texture, which the clerk assured her was excellent.

"A dollar and ninety-eight cents," she mused aloud. "Well, I'll take this pair." She handed the girl a five-dollar bill and waited for her change and for her parcel. What a very small parcel it was! It seemed lost in the depths of her shabby old shopping-bag.

Mrs. Sommers after that did not move in the direction of the bargain counter. She took the elevator, which carried her to an upper floor into the region of the ladies' waiting-rooms. Here, in a retired corner, she exchanged her cotton stockings for the new silk ones which she had just bought. She was not going through any acute mental process or reasoning with herself, nor was she striving to explain to her satisfaction the motive of her action. She was not thinking at all. She seemed for the time to be taking a rest from that laborious and fatiguing function and to have abandoned herself to some mechanical impulse that directed her actions and freed her of responsibility.

How good was the touch of the raw silk to her flesh! She felt like lying back in the cushioned chair and reveling for a while in the luxury of it. She did for a little while. Then she replaced her shoes, rolled the cotton stockings together and thrust them into her bag. After doing this she crossed straight over to the shoe department and took her seat to be fitted.

She was fastidious. The clerk could not make her out; he could not reconcile her shoes with her stockings, and she was not too easily pleased. She held back her skirts and turned her feet one way and her head another way as she glanced down at the polished, pointed-tipped boots. Her foot and ankle looked very pretty. She could not realize that they belonged to her and were a part of herself. She wanted an excellent and stylish fit, she told the young fellow who served her, and she did not mind the difference of a dollar or two more in the price so long as she got what she desired.

It was a long time since Mrs. Sommers had been fitted with gloves. On rare occasions when she had bought a pair they were always "bargains," so cheap that it would have been preposterous and unreasonable to have expected them to be fitted to the hand.

Now she rested her elbow on the cushion of the glove counter, and a pretty, pleasant young creature, delicate and deft of touch, drew a long-wristed "kid" over Mrs. Sommer's hand. She smoothed it down over the wrist and buttoned it neatly, and both lost themselves for a second or two in admiring contemplation of the little symmetrical gloved hand. But there were other places where money might be spent.

There were books and magazines piled up in the window of a stall a few paces down the street. Mrs. Sommers bought two high-priced magazines such as she had been accustomed to read in the days when she had been accustomed to other pleasant things. She carried them without wrapping. As well as she could she lifted her skirts at the crossings. Her stockings and boots and well fitting gloves had worked marvels in her bearing—had given her a feeling of assurance, a sense of belonging to the well-dressed multitude.

She was very hungry. Another time she would have stilled the cravings for food until reaching her own home, where she would have brewed herself a cup of tea and taken a snack of anything that was available. But the impulse that was guiding her would not suffer her to entertain any such thought.

There was a restaurant at the corner. She had never entered its doors; from the outside she had sometimes caught glimpses of spotless damask and shining crystal, and soft-stepping waiters serving people of fashion.

When she entered her appearance created no surprise, no consternation, as she had half feared it might. She seated herself at a small table alone, and an attentive waiter at once approached to take her order. She did not want a profusion; she craved a nice and tasty bite—a half dozen bluepoints, a plump chop with cress, a something sweet—a crème-frappée, for instance; a glass of Rhine wine, and after all a small cup of black coffee.

While waiting to be served she removed

her gloves very leisurely and laid them be-side her. Then she picked up a magazine and glanced through it, cutting the pages with a blunt edge of her knife. It was all very agreeable. The damask was even more spotless than it had seemed through the window, and the crystal more sparkling. There were quiet ladies and gentlemen, who did not notice her, lunching at the small tables like her own. A soft, pleasing strain of music could be heard, and a gen-tle breeze was blowing through the win-dow. She tasted a bite, and she read a word or two, and she sipped the amber wine and wiggled her toes in the silk stockings. The price of it made no difference. She counted the money out to the waiter and left an ex-tra coin on his tray, whereupon he bowed before her as before a princess of royal blood.

There was still money in her purse, and

her next temptation presented itself in the shape of a matinée poster.

It was a little later when she entered the theatre, the play had begun and the house seemed to her to be packed. But there were vacant seats here and there, and into one of them she was ushered, between brilliantly dressed women who had gone there to kill time and eat candy and display their gaudy attire. There were many others who were there solely for the play and acting. It is safe to say there was no one present who bore quite the attitude which Mrs. Sommers did to her surroundings. She gathered in the whole—stage and players and people in one wide impression, and absorbed it and enjoyed it. She laughed at the comedy and wept—she and the gaudy woman next to her wept over the tragedy. And they talked a little together over it. And the gaudy woman wiped her eyes and sniffled on a tiny square of filmy, perfumed lace and passed little Mrs. Sommers her box of candy.

The play was over, the music ceased, the crowd filed out. It was like a dream ended. People scattered in all directions. Mrs. Sommers went to the corner and waited for the cable car.

A man with keen eyes, who sat opposite to her, seemed to like the study of her small, pale face. It puzzled him to decipher what he saw there. In truth, he saw nothing—unless he were wizard enough to detect a poignant wish, a powerful longing that the cable car would never stop anywhere, but go on and on with her forever.

THE STORM

A Sequel to "At the 'Cadian Ball"

The leaves were so still that even Bibi thought it was going to rain. Bobinôt, who was accustomed to converse on terms of perfect equality with his little son, called the child's attention to certain sombre clouds that were rolling with sinister intention from the west, accompanied by a sullen, threatening roar. They were at Friedheimer's store and decided to remain there till the storm had passed. They sat within the door on two empty kegs. Bibi was four years old and looked very wise.

"Mama'll be 'fraid, yes," he suggested with blinking eyes.

"She'll shut the house. Maybe she got Sylvie helpin' her this evenin'," Bobinôt responded reassuringly.

"No; she ent got Sylvie. Sylvie was helpin' her yistiday," piped Bibi.

Bobinôt arose and going across to the counter purchased a can of shrimps, of which Calixta was very fond. Then he returned to his perch on the keg and sat stolidly holding the can of shrimps while the storm burst. It shook the wooden store and seemed to be ripping great furrows in the distant field. Bibi laid his little hand on his father's knee and was not afraid.

Calixta, at home, felt no uneasiness for their safety. She sat at a side window sewing furiously on a sewing machine. She was greatly occupied and did not notice the approaching storm. But she felt very warm and often stopped to mop her face on which the perspiration gathered in beads. She unfastened her white sacque at the throat. It began to grow dark, and suddenly realizing the situation she got up hurriedly and went about closing windows and doors.

Out on the small front gallery she had hung Bobinôt's Sunday clothes to air and she hastened out to gather them before the rain fell. As she stepped outside, Alcée Laballière rode in at the gate. She had not seen him very often since her marriage, and never alone. She stood there with Bobinôt's coat in her hands, and the big rain drops began to fall. Alcée rode his horse under the shelter of a side projection where the chickens had huddled and there were plows and a harrow piled up in the corner.

"May I come and wait on your gallery till the storm is over, Calixta?" he asked.

"Come 'long in, M'sieur Alcée."

His voice and her own startled her as if from a trance, and she seized Bobinôt's vest. Alcée, mounting to the porch, grabbed the trousers and snatched Bibi's braided jacket that was about to be carried away by a sudden gust of wind. He expressed an intention to remain outside, but it was soon apparent that he might as well have been out in the open: the water beat in upon the boards in driving sheets, and he went inside, closing the door after him. It was even necessary to put something beneath the door to keep the water out.

"My! what a rain! It's good two years

sence it rain' like that," exclaimed Calixta as she rolled up a piece of bagging and Alcée helped her to thrust it beneath the crack.

She was a little fuller of figure than five years before when she married; but she had lost nothing of her vivacity. Her blue eyes still retained their melting quality; and her yellow hair, dishevelled by the wind and rain, kinked more stubbornly than ever about her ears and temples.

The rain beat upon the low, shingled roof with a force and clatter that threatened to break an entrance and deluge them there. They were in the dining room—the sitting room—the general utility room. Adjoining was her bed room, with Bibi's couch along side her own. The door stood open, and the room with its white, monumental bed, its closed shutters, looked dim and mysterious.

Alcée flung himself into a rocker and Calixta nervously began to gather up from the floor the lengths of a cotton sheet which she had been sewing.

"If this keeps up, *Dieu sait* if the levees goin' to stan' it!" she exclaimed.

"What have you got to do with the levees?"

"I got enough to do! An' there's Bobinôt with Bibi out in that storm—if he only didn' left Friedheimer's!"

"Let us hope, Calixta, that Bobinôt's got sense enough to come in out of a cyclone."

She went and stood at the window with a greatly disturbed look on her face. She wiped the frame that was clouded with moisture. It was stiflingly hot. Alcée got up and joined her at the window, looking over her shoulder. The rain was coming down in sheets obscuring the view of far-off cabins and enveloping the distant wood in a gray mist. The playing of the lightning was incessant. A bolt struck a tall chinaberry tree at the edge of the field. It filled all visible space with a blinding glare and the crash seemed to invade the very boards they stood upon.

Calixta put her hands to her eyes, and with a cry, staggered backward. Alcée's arm encircled her, and for an instant he drew her close and spasmodically to him.

"*Bonté!*" she cried, releasing herself from his encircling arm and retreating from the window, "the house'll go next! If I only knew w'ere Bibi was!" She would not compose herself; she would not be seated. Alcée clasped her shoulders and looked into her face. The contact of her warm, palpitating body when he had unthinkingly drawn her into his arms, had aroused all the old-time infatuation and desire for her flesh.

"Calixta," he said, "don't be frightened. Nothing can happen. The house is too low to be struck, with so many tall trees standing about. There! aren't you going to be quiet? say, aren't you?" He pushed her hair back from her face that was warm and steaming. Her lips were as red and moist as pomegranate seed. Her white neck and a glimpse of her full, firm bosom disturbed him powerfully. As she glanced up at him the fear in her liquid blue eyes had given place to a drowsy gleam that unconsciously betrayed a sensuous desire. He looked down into her eyes and there was nothing for him to do but to gather her lips in a kiss. It reminded him of Assumption.

"Do you remember—in Assumption, Calixta?" he asked in a low voice broken by passion. Oh! she remembered; for in Assumption he had kissed her and kissed and kissed her; until his senses would well nigh fail, and to save her he would resort to a desperate flight. If she was not an immaculate dove in those days, she was still inviolate; a passionate creature whose very defenselessness had made her defense, against which his honor forbade him to prevail. Now—well, now—her lips seemed in a manner free to be tasted, as well as her round, white throat and her whiter breasts.

They did not heed the crashing torrents, and the roar of the elements made her laugh as she lay in his arms. She was a revelation in that dim, mysterious chamber; as white as the couch she lay upon. Her firm, elastic flesh that was knowing for the first time its birthright, was like a creamy lily that the sun invites to contribute its breath and perfume to the undying life of the world.

The generous abundance of her passion, without guile or trickery, was like a white flame which penetrated and found response in depths of his own sensuous nature that had never yet been reached.

When he touched her breasts they gave themselves up in quivering ecstasy, inviting his lips. Her mouth was a fountain of delight. And when he possessed her, they seemed to swoon together at the very borderland of life's mystery.

He stayed cushioned upon her, breathless, dazed, enervated, with his heart beating like a hammer upon her. With one hand she clasped his head, her lips lightly touching his forehead. The other hand stroked with a soothing rhythm his muscular shoulders.

The growl of the thunder was distant and passing away. The rain beat softly upon the shingles, inviting them to drowsiness and sleep. But they dared not yield.

The rain was over; and the sun was turning the glistening green world into a palace of gems. Calixta, on the gallery, watched Alcée ride away. He turned and smiled at her with a beaming face; and she lifted her pretty chin in the air and laughed aloud.

III

BOBINÔT AND BIBI, trudging home, stopped without at the cistern to make themselves presentable.

"My! Bibi, w'at will yo' mama say! You ought to be ashame'. You oughtn' put on those good pants. Look at 'em! An' that mud on yo' collar! How you got that mud on yo' collar, Bibi? I never saw such a boy!" Bibi was the picture of pathetic resignation. Bobinôt was the embodiment of serious solicitude as he strove to remove from his own person and his son's the signs of their tramp over heavy roads and through wet fields. He scraped the mud off Bibi's bare legs and feet with a stick and carefully removed all traces from his heavy brogans. Then, prepared for the worst—the meeting with an over-scrupulous housewife, they entered cautiously at the back door.

Calixta was preparing supper. She had set the table and was dripping coffee at the hearth. She sprang up as they came in.

"Oh, Bobinôt! You back! My! but I was uneasy. W'ere you been during the rain? An' Bibi? he ain't wet? he ain't hurt?" She had clasped Bibi and was kissing him effusively. Bobinôt's explanations and apologies which he had been composing all along the way, died on his lips as Calixta felt him to see if he were dry, and seemed to express nothing but satisfaction at their safe return.

"I brought you some shrimps, Calixta," offered Bobinôt, hauling the can from his ample side pocket and laying it on the table.

"Shrimps! Oh, Bobinôt! you too good fo' anything!" and she gave him a smacking kiss on the cheek that resounded. "*J'vous réponds*, we'll have a feas' to night! umph-umph!"

Bobinôt and Bibi began to relax and enjoy themselves, and when the three seated themselves at table they laughed much and so loud that anyone might have heard them as far away as Laballière's.

IV

ALCÉE LABALLIÈRE WROTE to his wife, Clarisse, that night. It was a loving letter, full of tender solicitude. He told her not to hurry back, but if she and the babies liked it at Biloxi, to stay a month longer. He was getting on nicely; and though he missed them, he was willing to bear the separation a while longer—realizing that their health and pleasure were the first things to be considered.

V

AS FOR CLARISSE, she was charmed upon receiving her husband's letter. She and the babies were doing well. The society was agreeable; many of her old friends and acquaintances were at the bay. And the first free breath since her marriage seemed to restore the pleasant liberty of her maiden days. Devoted as she was to her husband, their intimate conjugal life was something which she was more than willing to forego for a while.

So the storm passed and every one was happy.

COUNTERPOINTS